A Place to Hide

More **Strange Matter**™ from
Marty M. Engle & Johnny Ray Barnes Jr.

STRANGE MATTER

A Place to Hide

Johnny Ray Barnes, Jr.

A MONTAGE PUBLICATION

Montage Publications, a Front Line company,
San Diego, California

ISBN 1-56714-039-4

Printed in the U.S.A.

TO OUR FAMILIES
&
FRIENDS
(You know who you are.)

The whole thing seemed like a bad dream. Thinking back, twelve-year-old Trey Porter would never have guessed he could end up this way.

He settled into the tallest cedar he could find. The wind blew harder, making the tree sway frightfully. Trey thought about the fifteen minutes it had taken him to climb to his perch. Nothing, absolutely nothing, nature could throw at him was going to make him climb back down.

Not with those Things out there. Those Woodlizards.

Trey looked down. What if he fell asleep? At the very least he'd crash to the ground and break a couple of bones. That was nothing compared to what the Woodlizards would do to him, though. No, he wouldn't fall asleep. Trey doubted if he would ever sleep again.

He scanned the area around his tree, straining to hear even the quietest whisper. If a rat breathed, he would know it.

He was hungry, too. Really hungry. His stomach growled so loudly that Trey was sure the Woodlizards could hear it. He tried to keep his mind on other things. Like his parents.

But he might never see his mother again. Or his father. He considered this, too. Being trapped in one of the largest forests in the state, with Woodlizards after him, was definitely having a bad effect on Trey's outlook.

If he ever got this mess, Trey swore he would round up a posse and come hunt those Woodlizards down. He would find every rifle-toting hunter within the area and bring them out here to put an end to these fiendish creatures.

But would even hunters have a chance? Trey sure didn't want anyone to suffer the same fate his friends had. How would he ever be able to explain things to their families if he got out of here?

"When," Trey said aloud. When he got out of here. He had to think positively.

He had to find a way out. He had to escape.

The Woodlizards would find him soon. He would have to be prepared.

Trey strained to remember everything that had happened that day. Maybe he had overlooked something that could help him out of this mess. Something that could save him. Leaning his head back against a branch, he shut his eyes, and remembered.

Saturday morning began like any other day. After doing chores, Trey and his two best friends, Doug and Kevin, met at their camp site at the edge of the Dark Woods. For the last week, they'd planned on camping out Saturday night. They'd even come out and set up their tents right after school on Friday, so everything would be ready for the weekend.

They were joking around when Trey noticed the painted symbol on the flap of his tent. A skull and crossbones.

Waylon Burst. It had to be. The skull and crossbones was the mark of Waylon Burst, the meanest bully in Fairfield Junior High School. Somehow he'd found their campsite. That meant trouble, big trouble. He and his buddies would attack the campsite, tear it to pieces, then beat all them all to a pulp unless they were lucky enough to get away.

The three boys looked around nervously.

"It can't be," Kevin almost whined as his red, frizzy head blew in the wind. "Not here. Not this time."

"How could he have known?" Doug asked in his normal, squeaky voice, "We were so careful. No one knew we were camping here except our parents."

"Well, I'm sure they didn't say anything," Trey said. "They'd never tell Waylon. Not in a million years."

"Then how'd he find us?" Doug looked around nervously. "Oh, man. You know what this means. He's coming after us for sure."

"Well," Trey sighed, "there's always a risk of him finding out anytime we set up a camp. Waylon hates to see other kids having fun."

Trey knew what drove the bully to spoil things for everyone else. The story around school was that Waylon's dad, an ex-wrestler who ran the Fairfield garage, had been one of the biggest bullies in Fairfield's history when he was a kid. Sometimes Waylon brought proof that his dad was still that way, when he'd show up at school with assorted bruises or maybe a black eye. No wonder he'd turned out so mean.

"We're sitting ducks here," Doug said. "We're alone, no parents around. There's nothing to stop him from destroying everything, then stomping us."

"So what're we going to do?" Kevin asked.

Trey was tired of having to watch everything he did just because Waylon Burst might not like it.

"I say we make a stand. He's run us off from our last three camp sites. What do you say, Doug?"

"Waylon's big. I'm running." Doug caught the glasses slipping down his nose.

Kevin grunted in agreement.

Trey looked at them, and shook his head. He tried to rally his friends.

"Look, Waylon thinks we're easy targets 'cause of my weight, Doug's voice, and your hair, Kevin. If we make a stand, maybe he'll figure we're too much trouble to mess with, and leave us alone."

Doug and Kevin appeared to consider Trey's point for a moment. Then Doug turned to Kevin. "I know where there's an even better campsite."

Kevin nodded and began to take down his tent.

Trey's heart sank, even though he'd known things would end up this way. They always did. His friends wore their fear like painted-on leather jackets.

"So we're gonna give up everything we've built together?" he demanded loudly, following his friends a few steps.

"I'm not getting beat up over a patch of grass," Doug said. "Besides, I know a camp site Waylon will never find. Widow Hill."

Trey couldn't believe what he had just heard. Widow Hill.

A haunting legend surrounded that name. A legend of a great battle fought between Revolutionary War soldiers and a gang of pirates who ambushed them. A battle fought over some sort of magic prize the soldiers were protecting.

The soldiers had fallen back to the hill and held out for fourteen days until the pirates finally overwhelmed them. In those two weeks, they built a makeshift fort for cover.

Trey, like every other kid in Fairfield, heard the rumors that that fort still stood at the top of Widow Hill, but that's all Trey believed it to be, a rumor. It sure wasn't worth stomping all over the Dark Woods, something their parents forbade them to do anyway, just to search for some dumb fort that probably wasn't even there. Besides, Widow Hill, was over three hours away.

"That's too far to go," said Trey.

Kevin looked up from folding his tent. "What are you talking about, Trey? We've got all day. It'll only take us a couple of hours anyway."

"Our parents will kill us if they find out," Trey warned.

"Trey, if you did everything your parents told you to do, you'd still be in cub scouts. Now I've heard enough from my granddad to figure out how to find this place, and it'll be a kick to be able to tell everyone at school we camped there overnight."

Trey looked back at their campsite uncertainly. The skull on his tent flap seemed to be laughing at him. It still burned him to get run off by Waylon Burst, though.

Suddenly, birds scattered noisily from a hilltop a hundred yards away.

Doug and Kevin kicked up a storm of leaves as he took off into the Dark Woods.

Trey caught a glimpse of someone coming over the hill. It was Waylon Burst.

Doug and Kevin took off running, and the hunt began.

Waylon had brought his three henchmen; Wolf, Blade, and Count Nefarious. As soon as they saw Trey, they came after him like a shot.

Trey crashed into the woods after his friends, running for all he was worth. He swore revenge at the four bullies in between gasps for air. Who were these guys to break up his camp, anyway? Someday, he'd turn the tables on them. Right now, though, he had to concentrate on saving his skin.

Trey couldn't even see Doug and Kevin anymore. A lifetime of running away from bullies had prepared them well for things like this.

Waylon and his soldiers were gaining on Trey. All the snacks and fatty foods he'd eaten over the years were taking their toll, slowing him down and making him easy prey for his pursuers. It was getting harder to catch his breath, and jumping over obstacles was becoming nearly impossible.

Trey tried not to look back, but couldn't help himself. He couldn't see anyone behind him anymore! Maybe the other boys had given up the chase. No! He could still hear them crashing through the undergrowth. They were moving to surround him. He had to keep running.

The ground was getting more uneven and Trey had to really concentrate on where he was going. He looked up momentarily to find an escape route, and heard a splash.

His feet hit water.

He stumbled into puddle in an old stream bed. Desperately, he looked around and saw that the stream led into the mouth of a mud-walled trench.

No time to think about it. Trey headed for the trench.

Sprinting down the ditch, Trey looked up to his left and saw Wolf, the shortest of Waylon's friends, running with him step for step. Wolf was leering at Trey with an "I'm going to get you" look in his eyes. He called out to the other bullies that he had found one of their targets.

Trey's spirits rose momentarily when he noticed that the path in front of Wolf veered sharply away just ahead. His hopes were dashed, though, when Wolf, who saw the same thing, made a flying leap across the ditch to Trey's right, where he could continue the chase.

There was water in the trench, and Trey was splashing through it as he ran. Uh-oh. The water was getting deeper. Trey prayed it was simply rainwater that had settled into some dips in the ground, and that he wasn't running into a real creek. If he was, the chase would be over, and his goose would be cooked.

Out of the corner of his eye, Trey saw another figure appear on his left, where the path had once again veered next to the ditch. It was Blade. He was struggling to catch up, but the ground was muddy and he kept slipping.

"Just jump over," Wolf yelled at him.

Two more steps and Blade made his leap.

He didn't even come close to making it. Just as he took off, his foot slipped on the muddy ground and he crashed face first into the brackish water in the trench.

Trey didn't even slow down as he heard the

splash and scream behind him. He began to hope against hope that he might get away after all.

Ten yards later, that hope vanished.

The trench emptied into a scum-covered pond, and at its edge Trey came to a splashing halt. The water was over his knees.

Wolf stopped too, grinning down at his frazzled quarry.

Trey looked around desperately for a way out, but before he could find one he heard a loud splash to his right. Count Nefarious jumped in a few yards from him.

"Nowhere to run, Lard Butt," Nefarious sneered, moving in for the attack.

Trey backed further into the pond.

"Yeah, fat boy," Wolf cried from above. "Go in there. I bet there's all kinds of snakes and worms waiting for you. But that won't stop Nefarious. You're dead meat."

Trey backed in a couple of more steps. He stood about ten feet from his pursuers. The water was almost to his waist. It smelled horribly, with patches of green and brown slime floating on its surface. Unseen things swam and nibbled at his legs.

Just when it appeared things couldn't get

any worse, they did. Waylon and Blade, who was holding his chin gingerly from where he fell on it, appeared on the bank next to Wolf.

Waylon swaggered up to the edge of the foul swamp.

"Go in and get him," Waylon commanded.

Wolf was about to object when a voice screamed, "WHEN YOU THINK OF MUD FROM NOW ON, YOU'LL THINK OF DOUG KERVITZ!"

Trey's heart jumped to his throat. His friends! They hadn't deserted him after all. He turned slightly to see them standing defiantly on the left bank of the pond. Doug shouted again and hurled a huge mud ball at Nefarious. The missile smacked him right in the middle of his forehead. Another one, this time from Kevin, caught the bully's shoulder.

Trey's glee at seeing his friends pelting Nefarious was very short lived. Within seconds, the other three boys started tossing mud balls of their own. Being older and stronger, it didn't take long for their efforts to overwhelm Doug and Kevin. Then Doug slipped while stooping over to scoop up more mud. Reflexively, he grabbed on to Kevin. Both of them crashed into the pond near Trey.

The laughter from Waylon and his thugs was sickening. Trey wanted to drown them all.

"Get them," Waylon commanded once again.

As Wolf, Blade, and Count Nefarious waded toward them, Trey noticed a drainage pipe at the bottom of the bank where Doug and Kevin had been standing before they fell in. Trey shuddered when he imagined what might be in there, but it was their only way out. Shouting at his friends to follow, Trey splashed over to the pipe, bent down, and crawled in.

The pipe was pitch black inside. There were about four inches of the foulest smelling water Trey had ever come across on the bottom, but he paid it no mind as he crawled along. They had to get away from Waylon and the others. The inside walls of the pipe were covered in slime, making it difficult to make any progress. The boys kept going, anyway.

Trey raised his head cautiously and took a deep breath, trying not to gag on the horrible stench.

Kevin and Doug weren't quite as careful. Both of them bumped the top of the pipe when they tried to stand up. Kevin cried out, then slipped down into the water in the bottom of the pipe. The slimy liquid filled his open mouth when he fell. He came up sputtering and spitting, horrified at what he might have just swallowed.

"Take it easy, Kevin," Trey said. "Try to take deep breaths. That'll help you calm down."

Kevin coughed and hacked some more, but finally settled down.

Doug was too terrified to move. "We can't wait in here until they leave," he whimpered. "They'll be out there all night."

"We're not going to wait," Trey said with more courage than he felt. "We're going the rest of the way through this pipe."

"No way," Kevin almost shouted. "I'd rather get pounded by Waylon."

Trey's eyes had finally adjusted to the darkness. He could just make out the dim shapes of his friends.

"This pipe can't go on forever," Trey said, trying to convince the two boys. "Besides, we don't have any choice. Follow me."

With that, Trey took a deep breath and started down the pipe.

Reluctantly, Doug and Kevin followed.

They crawled for what seemed like an hour, although Trey was pretty sure it was probably a lot less than that, before they saw a feeble light.

An opening! It was at least five feet above

them, and there was water spilling in from it, but it was a way out.

"Why's there water coming in from there?" Kevin asked, sounding panicky.

"How should I know?" Trey responded testily. "Anyway, who cares? It's a way out."

"There's no ladder," Doug whined. "There should be a ladder. There's always a ladder on TV."

Trey thought for a moment.

"Here, give me a boost. Let's see where this thing goes."

Kevin moved over next to him, then laced his fingers together to give Trey a place to step up on. Trey placed his foot in Kevin's hands, but when he tried to step up, Kevin's fingers slipped apart, sending him crashing to the tunnel floor.

"Ouch!" Trey cried.

"It's all the slime on my hands, Trey," Kevin whined. "It makes them slippery."

"Okay, okay. I know. Doug, you come here and help, and we'll try again."

Kevin and Doug laced their hands together, and gripped each other as tightly as they could. Trey stepped onto their human step again. This time their grip held.

Trey reached up and grabbed hold of the edge

of the opening. He strained to pull himself up.

Doug and Kevin tried with all their might to lift Trey higher. Finally, with one massive grunt, they got him up high enough so Trey could get his elbows on the rim of the opening.

Trey wriggled and squirmed until he was finally able to work his way out of the hole.

It was pouring rain. That explained why there was so much water going into the pipe. A midday rain had hit the Dark Woods, and Trey realized it might very well drown his friends if he didn't do something quickly.

Amidst the torrent of rain falling around him, Trey could hear them yelping.

Lying on top of the tunnel's entrance, Trey reached one arm in as far down as he could. He felt someone grab onto his arm. Trey strained and pulled as hard as he could, lifting with all his might.

Kevin came up out of the pipe kicking and screaming. Trey swung him to saftey.

Both boys reached back in and grabbed onto Doug. They almost had him out of the hole, but he slipped and fell back into the pipe. They tried again, this time succeeding in dragging their friend out into the open air.

The three boys sat on top of the tunnel for a few minutes in the rain, catching their breaths and wondering what to do next.

They looked around and, despite the rain and what they had gone through to get there, found they were in a place that was actually quite peaceful.

A picturesque waterfall tumbled off the rocks on the far side of the small pond that lay in front of them. Kevin pointed to an opening in the rocks they could just make out under the waterfall. A shelter.

"We can walk around to it, or swim there in a couple of seconds."

Trey shuddered. He'd had enough water sports for a while. "Let's walk."

The crackle of fire was a sound Trey didn't like. His dad, a fireman in Fairfield, had taken him along on a couple of two alarm blazes. Trey remembered the sound of the flames, and how it made him afraid for his father. He thought about that when he lit the fire with one of the matches he'd kept in a sealed baggie in his pocket.

"Your dad teach you to keep matches like that?" Doug asked as he wrung the water out of his socks.

"Nah. I saw it on TV on the Discovery channel," Trey answered, putting more sticks on the blaze.

"How'd you know we'd make it through the tunnel?"

Trey shrugged. "I didn't. I figured we could at least hang out for a while until Waylon and his pals left. I never thought we'd actually have to go through it."

As Kevin laid his pants flat on a rock, he peered over at the open drain. He asked, "Hey, Trey. Why would anyone care about draining this lagoon anyway?"

Trey emptied some old snack wrappers from his pockets and tossed them on the fire. "I dunno. Pretty weird, huh?"

Doug stood up. "Those guys on the other side of the hill. What's to stop them from climbing over to this side and beating the tar out of us?"

"That hill's a mud slide. 'Sides, they don't know we're over here."

Trey just wanted to forget all about Waylon Burst and his gang. He sat back against the rocks and watched the rain through the waterfall. Pretty soon all he could think of was food.

Usually around one o'clock in the afternoon he'd be eating a second lunch.

Slowly, his friends began to transform before his eyes. Kevin became a corn dog smothered in mustard, and Doug became a cream filled donut. Trey's stomach gurgled and his mouth watered, then the stupid corn dog had to spoil everything by speaking.

"Hey, Trey, the sun's coming out."

Kevin became himself again as a shaft of sunlight beamed into their cozy little camp. Trey squinted and turned his head away so the light wouldn't blind him, and he noticed a hole in the back rock he hadn't seen before. When the sun shone on it, a green twinkling could be seen from inside.

"What's that?" he said loud enough to cause Doug and Kevin to turn and look.

They watched him as he walked over to the hole, and grabbed a long stick nearby. He poked it inside, but couldn't feel a bottom or sides to the hole. Then he stooped over and picked up a pebble, and tossed it in. Trey listened closely. It took several long seconds for the pebble to hit bottom.

"It's a cave, and something's in there."

Doug and Kevin stayed where they were.

"What do you mean 'something's in there'?" Kevin asked.

"I saw something reflect the sunlight." Trey examined the cave's opening a little more closely. It was way to small for him. "Hey, it's too small for me, but one of you guys..."

Kevin looked at him like he had lost his mind. "No way, dude. Are you nuts?" Doug nodded vigorously in agreement.

Trey just shrugged, then turned and stuck his head inside the hole. A blast of cold air hit him in the face.

"Well?" Doug cried. "What is it? What's down there?"

Darkness. Trey peered hard into the cave, but couldn't see anything.

"Hey, talk to us, Trey! What's in there?"

"I can't see anything," Trey said as he pulled his head out of the hole. He felt something crawling through his hair. Before he could move any further, Kevin and Doug screamed and began slapping him on the head.

"WHAT ARE YOU DOING?" Trey yelled, reaching out to punch one of the other boys at the time.

"NO, NO. IT'S SPIDERS. SPIDERS ON YOUR HEAD!" Kevin yelled.

Trey scrambled over to the waterfall and stuck his head under the icy stream. He saw little orange spiders with green dots on their backs washing into the pond. He wanted to scream, but concentrated on combing all the living things out of his hair instead. In his excitement, the baggie of matches dropped out of his pants

23

pocket and disappeared into the murky water.

Doug was rubbing his chin where Trey had connected with one of his wild swings. "Still want to stick your head in that hole, Trey?"

Trey growled back at him, then looked at the opening again. He really did want to know what was inside.

"Well, whatever's in there, it's covered with spiders, and I don't want anything to do with it," Doug said with finality. "We might at well start humping to Widow Hill." ·

"Widow Hill?" Trey responded in disbelief. "You still want to go to Widow Hill?"

"Well, yeah," Doug said, a little uncertainly. "We still need a campsite, don't we? We don't have the tents anymore, but hey, Widow Hill's a fort, remember? Gotta be shelter there. If we hurry we can still make it before dark."

"I don't know," Kevin mumbled. "Our parents won't know where we are. And we don't have any matches anymore, either. I saw Trey drop them."

"So we'll rub two sticks together. Come on!"

Trey couldn't help feeling uneasy. It'd be late in the day before they reached Widow Hill. There was also a very real chance of getting lost, since none of them knew exactly where they were going. He had an awful feeling they were making a big mistake.

The three friends moved deliberately up and down the mud covered hills. Often, one of them would slip or stumble and the others would have to stop and wait for him to catch up. The farther they went, the darker the woods seemed to grow, even though it was still full daylight.

"They say it's completely cut off from the rest of the world," Doug said as he pushed off against a small rock. The rock suddenly came loose and tumbled down the hill past Trey and Kevin.

"Hey, watch what you're doing!"

Doug ignored him and kept on climbing. "It'll be a fort that all other forts can only hope to be." He was oblivious to the trail of stones and twigs cascading down the slope behind him.

"Hey, Doug, if this place is so great, how come no one has ever claimed it before?"

"Because of the Things. People think there are Things up there."

Trey saw Kevin's eyes widen in surprise.

"WHAT THINGS? YOU NEVER TOLD US ABOUT ANY THINGS BEFORE!"

Doug looked back patiently. "Dead things, Kevin, dead things. Things that aren't supposed to be alive, but they are. Things that would eat you if they had a chance. Things that will chase you until you fall," he taunted.

"Trey." Kevin turned. "I don't think this fort's worth it."

"Relax," Doug said. "It's worth it. Those're only stories people made up, anyway. Some people even say the pirates are still up there looking for the loot they never found. My granddad says the ghosts of the soldiers still walk the woods, looking for revenge. I think it's all schnauzer kibble."

"So you're not scared?" Trey gulped for air as he caught up.

"Trey, my friend, I only fear things that are real. Things I know can hurt me, like a hot iron, or a sharp pencil, or Waylon Burst. Those things are real and dangerous. Monsters are not real."

Doug stopped suddenly.

"Hey, what's wrong?" Trey asked.

When Doug didn't respond, Trey trudged up the last few steps and stood next to him.

In front of them he saw a sinkhole, forty yards across, filled with the slimiest, reddest clay Trey had ever seen. Smack dab in the middle of the goo stood a lone tree.

"Okay, Doug, now what? Where's the fort?"

Doug looked around for a moment, then back at the sinkhole, then beyond it. He sighed.

"See that hill?" He was pointing to a rise just the other side of the sinkhole "The fort's just on the other side. As long as we stay on the edge of this gunk we should be okay. We'll be at the fort in no time."

"Doug," Trey said tiredly. "This fort definitely doesn't have what I would call easy access."

"Of course not," Doug replied. "That's to discourage enemies from attacking."

Someone spoke from behind them. "Oh, I wouldn't say that."

The boys turned to see the menacing form of Waylon Burst smirking at them. Wolf, Blade, and the Count appeared from the trees and surrounded the clay pool.

Kevin panicked when the four bullies started toward them. He turned to run toward Widow Hill, stepping into the the reddish goo in his haste to get away. His foot disappeared into the muck. He shouted for Trey and Doug to help him, but before either boy could move toward him...

The forest around them seemed to begin to shake.

Then snarls and growls filled the air.

Waylon Burst screamed.

Around the clay pool, they appeared.

The Things.

Trey only caught a glimpse of the Things before he ran, but the image of what he saw was burned into his brain.

Monsters. Living, breathing monsters with four legs, thick undulating bodies, and short pointed tails.

They were green, and covered in scales. Reptilian, like lizards, but with longer legs. They had teeth, and hissed as they moved in to attack all the boys.

The monsters emerged from the woods in every direction and surrounded the entire sinkhole.

Trey had never moved so fast in his life. Every sound he heard spurred him on. When he reached the side of the claypool, he clawed frantically at the walls, trying to climb out. He heard the others screaming behind him, and felt the

Things getting closer.

Trey groped for the top of the wall, trying to find something to pull himself up, but grabbed nothing but fungus. Finally, he grasped a stump and dug his fingers tightly into it. Ants swarmed over his hand as he used every ounce of strength to lift himself to the top, and onto the upper bank. As he pulled his feet over the edge, he heard something hiss. He felt hot breath against his leg. Trey assumed one of those things had jumped up for him and missed. He didn't waste any time wondering.

He heard awful cries and screams from both friends and enemies in the background as he tore through the brush, looking for a way out. What could he do for them now?

At the moment, he didn't care. Any turn he made could be fatal. Every stump in his path could trip him, sealing his fate. He felt sure those things were coming after him. He had to get away. He had to find a place to hide.

The fort!

Doug had said the fort was just on the other side of the hill, but Trey couldn't see any sign of it. If Widow Hill really existed at all, he was probably well past it by now. He leapt over dead branches and trenches, looking vainly for the relic.

Then he heard a terrible shriek a few yards behind him. The Things were closing in.

Trey didn't care where he went now. He just wanted to get away.

He ran to the bottom of a hill, where he had to pause for a few seconds to catch his breath. Then he heard screams back in the woods. Trey couldn't tell if the shrieks belonged to Doug, or to Kevin, or either.

"No, this can't be happening," Trey muttered. "It can't be." Tears welled up in his eyes, but he forced them back down.

He looked around for a hole to crawl into, or some bushes to crawl under. Then he saw it in the distance.

A good three hundred yards away. Nothing grew there; no bushes, no weeds, no trees. At the top, he saw something made of stone and wood. And at the moment it looked like the safest place in the world.

"Widow Hill," Trey whispered. "I've found it!"

But something had found him. Something that came to a stop just behind him. He didn't have to turn. He heard it spit and hiss as he got to his feet. Then it laughed.

Trey ran, and heard the Thing's feet slapping the ground behind him. It panted like a race horse. So did Trey. He ran to Widow's Hill thinking it would be his last chance.

He had to get to the peak. He didn't know what he would do when he got there, but at the moment it looked like the only place to run. The thing closed in on him as he hit the base of Widow Hill and started his ascent.

Like everything else Trey had encountered in the forest that day, the hill was muddy and slick. He had to grab at stones every few feet to keep himself from sliding back down the hill. He clawed his way desperately up the slope.

With the spitting beast almost on him, Trey jerked his head around to see its face.

The teeth. Before he saw anything else, he saw the teeth. Terribly long ones, white from the tip to the pink gums, packed into the scaled mouth of something unbelievably horrible.

The eyes! They glowed a fiery red! Trey slumped, mesmerized by the eyes as the Thing prepared to attack.

But something came out of the ground before that could happen.

A long sharp blade, tied to the end of a rifle, emerged from the dirt just a foot away from Trey's head. The pointed edge came to rest at the side of the beast's neck. Trey looked to see what held the rifle, and screamed again.

A decayed skeleton had the rifle in a tight, bony grip.

"Goodbye, Pogue," the skeleton said in a rattling voice.

The beast lifted its head and howled in anger, then retreated down the hill.

The skeleton turned to Trey, who, still unable to move, continued to scream.

"Now," spoke the frame of bones. "What do we do with you...?"

Trey kicked and screamed and cried as the skeleton grabbed him by the legs, and pulled him into the hole in the earth it had just emerged from. Dirt got into his eyes before Trey could close them. He was afraid to see what would happen next. Within a few short seconds, the skeleton pulled him through another opening, and tossed him onto a flat, dirt surface.

Trey coughed. Some of the dirt found its way into his mouth. Then he rubbed his stinging eyes, rose unsteadily to his feet, and looked around. Through tear-filled vision he saw an opening that led out of whatever room he was in. He ran for it.

Before he made it even three steps, the thing grabbed him again, jerking him back into the room. He fell flat on his chest, knocking all the air from his lungs. He couldn't even scream when the skeletal terror dragged him back into its dwelling.

Trey felt something clamped onto his ankle. Looking down at his foot, he saw his ankle had been cuffed to a cannonball, and that cannonball latched to another. All together he counted four. Noises from the opening caught his attention. The skeletal thing came back in, dressed in a very old hat and jacket, carrying the same rifle as before. A sword hung from its belt.

"I shall return," it said, and disappeared through a doorway.

"Where are you going?" Trey sobbed, "You can't leave me down here like this! You can't!"

Trey felt his aching stomach growling at him for not filling it on schedule. He'd already missed two meals. He figured his captor didn't have any need for food or water. At least, he couldn't see any evidence of either as he looked around the room.

Trey could just make out the sound of crickets chirping from somewhere above, so he figured it must be nighttime.

His last thought before he closed his eyes from exhaustion was that if the skeleton didn't return to let him go, he would surely die there.

Something dropped onto Trey's head, waking him shortly afterwards. At first he thought it was water, but then it started to move.

He let out a horrified cry, and shook his head vigorously, and scraped at his scalp to free it of the unwanted visitors.

A few seconds later, Trey heard something coming into the room. He couldn't stop himself from shaking in fear.

"You are the biggest coward I've ever seen," said a commanding voice through the walls of the hole.

That shut Trey up.

"I've fought beside boys your age in battle," the voice continued. "None of them have ever cried so much in the face of danger."

Trey's eyes grew wide and he yanked furiously at the chain as the skeleton came around the corner.

"P-Please don't hurt me," he pleaded as his eerie captor pulled a wooden crate to the middle of the room and sat down.

"Tell me, boy, why are you here?"

Trey tried to speak, but only a squeak came out.

"Water. You need water. I have a well. Answer me and I'll get you some."

"I was chased," Trey gasped. "I was chased by some bullies, and then by those Things. When I ran up here, you grabbed me."

The skeleton leaned in, and studied Trey's pale face.

"So you were alone?"

Trey decided not to hide anything.

"I had...have two friends. But those Things got them. I don't know what happened to them."

The bony figure stood, and looked down at the quivering Trey.

"I know what happened to them, and when I get back, I'll tell you."

With that, Trey's jailer left the room. He was gone for quite awhile. Trey shook his head, trying to think clearly, but things were just too bizarre to make sense.

Finally, Trey heard the familiar sound of dragging boots that preceded the weird creature's entrance. When it came around the corner, it carried a bucket of sloshing water. He dunked in a ladle and offered it to Trey. Trey gulped the rank fluid down greedily.

"I am a man...of my word," spoke the creature. "Are you, young man, a person of your word?"

Trey nodded.

"If I unlock these chains, will you try to run away?"

Trey shook his head. The skeleton took a key from his coat pocket, and unlocked the manacle around Trey's ankle.

Trey's first thought was to run, and to forget all about this place. But he had given his word, so he went with his instincts, and stayed.

"Who are you?" Trey asked.

The skeleton sat back on his crate, and pulled a pipe from his pocket. He lit it with a match. The skeleton went through the motion of inhaling, but with no lungs, the smoke simply crept over his face and through his eyes. Trey wondered why the thing even tried at all.

"It's a habit of mine that I never bothered to stop," the skeleton said. "You see, I need something to remind me I was once human."

The skeleton held the pipe at a distance and studied it. "I grew this tobacco here, myself. And the water you drank came from my underground well. I bored through rock to dig it, but that was a long time ago, when I needed water. I don't have much use for the wet stuff now. I suppose I was too proud of the well to cover it up. "

The skeleton looked around for a second, appearing to study the underground chamber.

"I made this place into a dwelling as well as a stronghold. I cannot leave here. This is where I've been for over two hundred years," the skeleton said and turned to Trey. "My name is Thomas Middleton."

THE HISTORY OF THE SPHERE

In 1776, America entered in a conflict with Britain known in history as the Revolutionary War. Thomas Middleton served as a soldier in that war. One night, a General ordered Thomas and another soldier, Ben Thumb, to his estate for a secret meeting. The American troops had suffered several defeats at the hands of the British, and they desperately needed new ideas to win the war.

The General explained that he'd received many letters from a man who claimed to have a weapon which would not only put an end to that war, but all wars. Thomas and Ben's mission would travel far to the west to this man's home, and bring the weapon back to Virginia. The trip would take several months.   After making preparations, Thomas and Ben set off.

The journey was long and hard, with both British soldiers and Indians making it even more dangerous.   Their food rations ran out quickly. Nearly starved, they reached their destination two weeks later than planned.

They rendezvoused with a young boy who called himself Jobe, who told them that the man they sought called himself the Keeper, and he would take them to him. They made the trip by boat, which took another day. Finally, they reached the Keeper's place at dawn, a hut built in the center of a swamp. On the dock, awaiting them, stood the Keeper.

When Thomas offered his hand in friendship, the Keeper stared at it, and then warily shook it.

The man's eyes had a very wise look about them. They reminded Thomas of his grandfather, someone who has seen all there was to see.   He decided this man could be trusted.

When they entered the Keeper's shack, Thomas asked about the weapon, but Ben asked anxiously for food. The Keeper decided to show them the weapon first. He motioned for the boy to retrieve it, and from under an old bed the boy pulled a locked iron box.

Producing a golden key from his pocket, the Keeper unlocked the box. When he lifted the lid, the room was instantly bathed in a soothing, green glow.

The Keeper pulled out a large, very green globe. It had a bright aura, and sent out vibrations that could be felt in the air like sparks of electricity. Thomas looked uneasily at Ben.

The Keeper motioned for Jobe to come close. Writing something down on paper, the Keeper showed his note to the boy. The boy closed his eyes, and placed his hands on the globe. Immediately, Thomas and Ben saw things popping up all around them.

Food.

In every corner of the shack appeared something that could be eaten. A turkey leg materialized in the flower pot, a cake on the bed, vegetables in the washpot, and more. The shack rapidly filled with mouth-watering aromas.

Jobe explained that the sphere knew the first desire of whomever touched it, and made that desire a reality. The note the Keeper had written to Jobe told him to think of nothing but food as he touched the sphere. It could only be used once by each person, and that wish had been Jobe's first.

This would be the weapon he would give to the Revolutionaries. He would not reveal how he came to possess it.

Armed with what they believed to be the greatest weapon in the world, the two soldiers prepared to leave the next day.

As Jobe helped Thomas and Ben get ready, Ben suggested they use the sphere to get them safely home, in an instant. Jobe gave them one last piece of information, the sphere's boundary. If you desired to be in another place, the sphere would put you there, but it would not come with you. Thomas and Ben took Jobe's word for it, and departed.

The two soldiers were prepared to guard the globe with their lives on the long trip back, but they made it only a little ways before their resolve was tested. Just as they reached Widow Hill, near what would later become the town of Fairfield, they were ambushed by pirates, who had heard of the secret weapon and followed the soldiers. Morley, Pogue, and Fitzgerald McCree, they claimed to be, and they attacked the

General's agents ferociously.

Badly wounded, Thomas and Ben escaped to the top of hill. They held the pirates off for fourteen days. With Ben hurt the worst, Thomas built a fort for shelter.

On the fourteenth day, Ben knew he was near death. He grabbed the sphere, and desiring nothing but revenge, pictured in his mind the hideous things he believed the McCrees to be.

As Ben passed on, Thomas heard screams, and looked into the valley to see the evil Things that the pirates had become. Scared out of his wits and agonized by his wounds, Thomas grabbed the sphere with only one thought on his mind; to simply keep on living.

That was two hundred years ago, and the Things were still out there. "Woodlizards" Thomas called them. All that time Thomas had been there guarding the sphere. If the Woodlizards ever got it, it might mean the end of the world. Thomas Middleton could never let that happen. He had become the sphere's new Keeper.

11

Trey stood up, looking at Thomas, and then around the rest of dwelling. The story seemed so unbelievable that it made Trey accept and forget at the same time the strange apparition before him. Somewhere close by surged the power to have anything he wanted, but he couldn't see it. Searching for a trace of green light, he found nothing.

"Where is it now?" Trey asked. "Where's the sphere?"

Thomas scratched at his skull, then hacked like he might be choking, which must have been a habit, since he had no lungs to cough with.

"No one will ever discover where it is. No one will ever see it," Thomas rasped.

"You've destroyed it?" Trey gasped. "With

that thing, I could have..."

"You could have what?"

Tough question. However, Trey felt sure he could answer it. The most constructive desire would be rescue. Or food. Or wishing Doug and Kevin home safely. All of these seemed like good things to wish for.

"A helicopter," he blurted. Thomas tilted his head in a questioning manner, and Trey explained. "With a helicopter, we could fly beyond the forest, to the city, and we could destroy the Woodlizards on the way out of here."

Thomas looked Trey's way, but his eyeless sockets gave no clue about his thoughts. When he shook his head, Trey feared the worst.

"You don't understand, boy," Thomas said, "You can't leave here. Not ever."

Trey was speechless.

"But you won't do me any good chained up down here. So, you'll help me guard the great sphere. Tonight, boy, will be your first watch."

Trey sat atop the old stone fort, smelling the wild Things that watched him from the dark. They were there, he knew.

"They know you're scared," rumbled Thomas as he stepped up out of the fort with a steaming bowl of something that smelled awful. Trey caught a glimpse of it, a thick bubbling concoction that produced orange and green swirls. It made Trey think of what was being served at his house on that night. Every Saturday, his mom served her famous meat loaf.

"I want to go home," Trey said nervously. He didn't want to believe Thomas would keep him there forever. Just the thought of being there on that hill for all eternity, with an undead soldier and a host of Woodlizards, was enough to make Trey scream.

"They'll grab you within the first two hundred yards if you try to run. The Woodlizards never go away."

Trey turned his attention to the bubbling mixture in the pot. Thomas offered him a spoon, and Trey tasted it. Much to his surprise, he found he liked it.

"Some of the roots around here are edible. I picked a few, and threw in some other herbs. It's what I survived on when I had to eat." He watched Trey scarf down the entire bowl. "Tell me, are all the young boys out there like you? Are they all fat?"

Trey stopped spooning the root soup into his mouth. For the first time, he looked straight into Thomas' eye sockets and didn't flinch.

"Are all Revolutionary War soldiers so thin?" he asked.

Thomas chuckled, then stiffened when he heard a noise from the woods.

Trey jumped behind the wall.

As the old soldier scanned the Dark Woods, Trey peeked over to look, too. He couldn't see anything.

"If they attack us and win, will they eat us?" Trey asked.

"I'm not sure what they eat, but it's not humans. When they attack humans, they turn that person into one of them. That victim joins the pack. They don't want strangers coming into the woods and stumbling on the sphere. This way, they turn enemies into allies."

"They turn into Woodlizards?" Trey asked anxiously. "Do you think that's what happened to my friends?"

Thomas nodded.

Trey was hopeful for a moment. Maybe Doug and Kevin weren't dead after all. But then he started thinking about the sickening details.

"How do they do it? How do they turn a person into a Woodlizard?"

"I've seen them do it once in two hundred years. It's a gruesome act, and not one you'd want to hear about. I don't even like to think too much about what they do out there. They attack this hill, and I run them off, and that's about it. I don't think I've seen their leader, Fitzgerald McCree, in fifty years," Thomas said.

"What happened to him?" Trey asked.

Thomas shrugged, as much as a skeleton could shrug. "He might have gotten tired of trying to get the sphere. Or maybe the rains got him. Rain, or water in general, kills them, you know. Even their bones dissolve in it."

Trey's spirits lifted a bit. It had rained on and off all through the day, and would probably continue to do so through the night Then he remembered Kevin and Doug. If they had changed into Woodlizards, he didn't want the rains to get them.

"What about my friends?" Trey asked again. "What can I do about them?"

"Let them go. The Woodlizard's curse is forever, or until the Woodlizard victim dies. They're part of the pack now, and I believe that puts the Woodlizard number at fifteen. There have been other lone travelers who met the same fate as your friends. But like I said, the rains take a few of them every year."

Horror swept over Trey as he thought about the terrible lives his friends had in store for them. A tugging guilt reminded him that he was the only one to escape, leaving his friends to live in the woods as monsters. He pitied Doug and Kevin, but he shivered when he thought that he could easily be in their place.

"I don't want to end up like my friends," Trey said.

"Keep your guard up boy, and you won't have to."

Trey heard a low growl. He looked over Thomas' shoulder to see one of the Woodlizards in mid air.

It knocked Thomas off his seat, and Trey thought the old soldier would surely fall apart as he hit the ground. The Woodlizard rolled with him, biting and spitting.

Trey had to do something. Picking up the nearest rock, he launched it in the direction of the squabble, hoping he wouldn't hit Thomas. He didn't. It struck the Woodlizard in the head. It stopped and turned to Trey.

Trey threw another rock, one even larger than the first. He found his target again. The green, scaly beast stumbled, and its eyes began to roll.

"Ah, Trey, why did you have to do that?" the monster said, then fell to the ground with a thud.

Doug's voice!

Trey's heart jumped in his chest, then sank to the pit of his stomach. It had happened. Thomas' awful prediction had come true, and Trey could do nothing but whimper a plea.

"D-Doug, are you okay?" Trey sobbed.

"Curse me for being a polite host." Thomas rose and grabbed his musket. "Instead of guarding the fort, I've been cooking for you. Well, you only knocked this one out. I'll see that he never wakes up." Thomas put the gun's barrel up to the Woodlizard's head.

"NO! DON'T DO IT!" Trey shouted, running forward to stop him. "THAT'S MY FRIEND! MY FRIEND DOUG!"

"Well, he's an ugly, hissing glowing-eyed lizard now, and there's no place for him in this world," Thomas yelled back.

A voice came from behind them. "The same could be said for a skeleton that walks."

Creeping over to the fort were four more Woodlizards.

Thomas turned to Trey. "Run!"

13

Trey did, without question. He could hear the beasts attacking behind him, but he never looked back. He heard the gun go off a few times and heard Thomas' curses and battlecries. Then Trey thought he heard Kevin's voice.

"I've got him! He's mine!" The call came from behind him.

Definitely Kevin.

Trey never dreamed there'd be a day that he ran from his friend, but now Kevin had four legs outnumbering his two.

"Join the pack, Trey. You'll be stronger than you ever were in your life," yelled the monster. The words were not Kevin's, but the sound of the voice certainly was.

Trey tore up a treacherous hill, picking up a number of cuts and bruises along the way. At the top, he looked down. Kevin was struggling to get up the hill and couldn't maintain the chase.

Trey sighed in relief, then heard something on his right.

More Woodlizards!

Trey took off.

Darting in and out of the trees, Trey could see more Woodlizards out of the corners of his eyes. They were surrounding him. It would be over soon.

Then he came to the rocks, a wall of stone leading up to another level of the Dark Woods. He jumped up and dug his fingers into the first groove he could find. Trey climbed it quickly, knocking down loose rocks with his feet, and hoping a few would hit his trackers on their heads.

The Woodlizards stopped at the wall and began to jump in the air. They couldn't climb the rocks. Trey almost laughed out loud, then realized that if he fell, they would catch him.

So he moved away slowly and carefully. He had never been much of a climber. His weight always slowed him down, but he wasn't going to let that stop him now. Looking up, he could see there were about another ten feet to go to safety.

He grabbed a rock to pull himself up, but it came loose in his hand.

"No, no, no, no, no!" he yelled.

Instinctively, he grabbed a plant that grew between the rocks.

It held.

Panting, he took hold of another rock, more cautiously than before.

Finally, he reached the top, and pulled himself onto level ground. He looked down, estimating he had just climbed twenty feet. Below him, the Woodlizards spit in disgust.

"That's the fastest I've ever seen him move," said the Kevin-lizard, who had caught up with the pack.

Trey continued to breathe heavily, wondering what he would do next. Then he felt the first drops of rain.

Trey remembered it all.

As soon as it started to rain, he had climbed into the leafy branches of a nearby tree, ignoring his father's warnings about lightning. What was lightning compared to the Woodlizards?

He saw the Woodlizards circling the ground below him, now that the rain had stopped. They apparently hadn't thought to look up into the tree for him.

They trotted through the trees for a few moments, then took their search deeper into the dark forest.

Trey knew they'd never give up.

He had to find his way out.

Trey also thought a lot about his friends. Somehow, someway, he had to save them. He still felt guilty, even more so since escaping from the fort. He'd left his friends in bad shape back there, including Thomas.

He shivered when thinking of the old soldier.

Did he consider Thomas a friend? Did he actually care what happened to a ghoul who kept him chained in a hole?

Run, Thomas had said. He had wanted Trey to get away. Yes, he wondered what had happened to Thomas. And the sphere.

The Woodlizards wanted the sphere so they can return to human form. But the Woodlizards still circled the woods, therefore they didn't have the sphere.

And if they didn't have it, then...

It must not have been at the fort at all.

Why would Thomas sit on top of a hill for two hundred years guarding nothing? Had it all been a lie? An interesting thing to consider.

Then Trey remembered the shiny thing in the cave by the waterfall.

"No way! That's it. "

It would be a brilliant strategy on Thomas' part. He must have somehow made his way to the falls with the sphere, hidden it there, but continued to guard the fort. The Woodlizards would still believe it to be in the fort. They would never think to look anywhere else. At least until they searched the fort. But not finding it there, the only thing to think about would be...

Me. The beasts think I have their sphere.

He heard a snap.

Trey looked across the way, at a tree about fifty yards from him. A branch broke and something, no, SOMEONE fell to the ground as Trey watched. The person hit the ground with a thud, and didn't move.

15

Trey could hardly contain himself. He had not expected to see anyone again, at least not until he escaped the woods.

The timing could not have been worse, with the Woodlizards roaming the area. They'd patrolled that section only moments before.

Trey didn't think twice. He lowered himself from the tree, looked around, and walked slowly over to the person who had fallen.

The crumpled mass twitched a bit, and let out with a moan.

Trey felt a familiar sense of dread tug at chest but couldn't figure out why until he reached the body.

When he saw who it was, his heart stopped, and he felt so dizzy that he almost fell back on his rear.

"H-Help me..." pleaded Waylon Burst.

Even though Waylon lay helpless before him, waiting to be paid back for all the suffering he'd inflicted, Trey was just too happy to see another human being to think about revenge.

Trey dropped to his knees as he finally realized he was passing up the best chance he'd probably ever have to get back at Waylon Burst. He drew in his breath, and turned Waylon over.

"I-I think I broke my ankle," Waylon whimpered. "Or maybe a sprain."

In the distance, Trey heard rustling in the brush. Something was coming.

"We've got to get out of here!"

Tears appeared in the corners of Waylon's eyes. Trey looked around desperately, finally spying a creek in the moonlight. He made a snap decision.

Trey muttered, "Sorry," grabbed Waylon by the arms, and dragged him toward the creek.

Waylon screamed. If his ankle truly was broken, it would never be the same after this. Trey figured every bump must have felt like an electric shock to the bully. It was rough going, because Waylon weighed much more than Trey'd guessed. The fact that he kept squirming in pain didn't help.

If Woodlizards didn't like water, they definitely wouldn't jump into a creek.

Ten feet from the water, the first Woodlizard emerged from the woods. Its eyes glowed red in the night, and its breath puffed from its mouth like a steam engine.

Waylon screamed even louder, and higher. He sounded like a girl.

With a mighty tug, Trey pulled them both into the water, falling backward as he did so.

The Woodlizard approached, followed by two more, walking slowly, stalking the boys.

Trey pulled Waylon deeper until they stood in the center of the creek, in freezing water up to their necks. If Trey's gamble about the water proved wrong, they'd be easy prey.

16

Trey's arms and legs were numb from the cold. He could barely hold onto Waylon, who kept whimpering loudly. The Woodlizards glared at them from the bank.

"If you know where the sphere is, tell us now. Otherwise, you'll stay in the creek all night, and we'll be here watching you freeze, or drown, whichever comes first," promised one of the hissing beasts.

Trey backed up slowly, meaning to exit the creek from the other side. To his horror, he saw another Woodlizard emerge on the other shore, growling and chuckling at the same time. Trey and Waylon were trapped.

Trey wished fiercely that he really had the sphere. He would wish for his Dad to roll up in a tank and blow these beasts away. But he didn't have any magic. He had nothing but his wits, and even those began to leave him as the cold numbed his brain, too. Then, as more Woodlizards came out of the hills, it suddenly dawned on him where he stood.

The creek! The creek that flowed down the mountain. The creek that emptied down the waterfall. The waterfall that housed the cave. *And the sphere.*

Trey whispered to Waylon, "Hang on, Waylon. We're going downstream."

The Woodlizards went after them, running alongside, jumping over rocks or stumps. The monsters seemed determined to follow them to the end.

"We're goners," Waylon moaned. "We can't stay in here forever. They'll get us for sure."

"If we can last until another storm hits, we'll be all right." Trey sounded steady, even in the cold temperature.

"We'll freeze before then, dude," murmured Waylon.

Trey looked at the Woodlizard who was following them. He recognized the monster by the knot on its head; Doug.

"We've got you Trey," Doug-lizard said. "Give us the sphere now. You don't have the guts to use it. "

Trey stared at him. What do you say to a friend once he's been turned into an evil creature and wants to see you dead? Trey said nothing as he watched lightning flash across Doug's green scaled body.

With the threat of rain, the pack gradually dropped back, and soon the only Woodlizard left was Doug. He followed along the bank, watching, waiting.

"Trey, if you've got the sphere, change me back," Doug-lizard pleaded. "Change me back."

Trey didn't respond. They looked at each other a moment longer before Doug finally retreated into the woods. Trey and Waylon floated, waiting for the rain so Trey would pull them both out.

Then Trey heard the waterfall.

17

The current became rougher. Realizing what lay ahead, Trey tried desperately to get to the side.

He lost his grip on Waylon, and the other boy sank beneath the water.

Trey dove after him.

The water was so black and murky he had to grope for the bully. Just when he was about to give up, he felt the leather jacket.

Yanking with all his strength he pulled the older boy to the surface.

They were still moving toward the fall.

At the last moment, Trey grabbed a small rock to anchor himself.

It came loose in his hands.

Trey started to go over the waterfall.

Something grabbed his shirt and held him

as he hung halfway over the falls.

Waylon.

The bully had some strength left.

With one arm, he pulled Trey onto a large boulder, and both of them hung on and rested for a second.

Then Waylon moved to the side of the creek and climbed out.

He held his hand out to Trey.

Trey was amazed.

Waylon had returned the favor, and saved his life.

"What do we do now?" Waylon asked in a sobbing breath.

"Can you walk?"

Waylon nodded.

"Then we head for the bottom of the falls. I know a place there."

18

Trey led the way to the makeshift camp he and Doug and Kevin had made earlier that day.

Trey felt funny being there with Waylon. He had ruined every camp the boys ever set up.

"I'm glad I left this one standing," Waylon said as he sat down heavily.

Waylon groaned as he took off his boot.

"How's your foot? Trey asked.

"Sprained. Cold water helped it."

Trey still saw fear in Waylon's eyes, and bet the other boy had never been this scared in his life.

"You hungry?" Waylon asked.

Food!

"Berries and leaves. Scavenged 'em earlier. Want some?"

Trey grabbed what Waylon offered. It

tasted like a very rough salad, but he was hungry enough to eat a horse.

Waylon looked in the direction of the large mud bank that Trey and his friends had crawled through via the pipe. If they climbed that bank, they could make it out of the woods in a matter of minutes.

"Those Things hate water, huh? Do you think if it started raining again we could make it home before they jumped us?"

"Probably," Trey said. "Until then, we're surrounded by water, and the monsters couldn't climb down here if they had to. Not without falling in."

Trey decided not to bring the secret of the sphere up yet. Waylon might not know. No matter how much Trey wanted to, he still wasn't sure he could trust Waylon. But keeping that secret was eating Trey up inside.

"How'd you learn to do all this?" Trey asked. "All about the berries and stuff? Do you watch the Survival Channel?"

Waylon looked up. "Nope. I was a Boy Scout for awhile."

That sent Trey's mind spinning. Waylon went on to tell him that he didn't care for the

Boy Scout motto, to be friendly to everyone, so he went renegade. He decided to live up to a long time family tradition and become a bully.

Could Trey trust this guy?

Waylon had saved his life, but could Trey trust him with a fantastic secret?

"How'd you get away?" Trey asked.

"Climbed a tree. And you?"

"I found the Widow Hill fort. I hid out there."

There, he said it. He'd made the commitment to trust Waylon Burst.

"No kidding. What'd you find?"

Trey leaned in.

"If we could save everyone, my friends and your guys too, would you do it?"

"I don't know. What do you mean 'save them'?" Waylon asked.

"Waylon, those monsters, some of them are our friends."

"Our friends? How?"

"It's a long story, but listen. I know something that can change them all back. I think it's in that cave."

Trey motioned to the dark hole and Waylon looked over at it. Trey thought he saw the bully shiver.

"What is it?" asked Waylon.

"Something magical."

Waylon jumped up and started pacing, then leaned against a rock to take the weight off his foot. It must still have been sore. His body relaxed.

Finally he asked, "How do you know all this stuff?"

If Waylon was ready to listen, Trey was ready to explain.

Trey shared every detail of his adventure with Waylon, from his captivity at the fort, a mutual trust with Thomas, and to his eventual escape.

"So these Things are our friends, but they've been turned into monsters?"

"Woodlizards. Yes, and that's what they'd do to us if they caught us. Once you're a Woodlizard, you follow the desire of the pack. They want to locate the sphere, and to keep anyone else from finding it."

"And a skeleton told you all this?"

"Thomas Middleton. The sphere cursed him with immortality. He told me most everything, and some of it I figured out on my own."

Waylon looked over at the hole.

"So you think the sphere's in there?"

"It would make sense. If the Woodlizards

think that the sphere's in the fort, then it would be a smart move to hide it somewhere else. Plus, this place is surrounded by water, except where we crawled down, and the Woodlizards aren't agile enough to climb down without falling into the drink. The only thing I can't figure out is how Thomas got it here without the Things seeing him."

"Maybe you're wrong," said Waylon, and then looked out into the dark. "It's going to rain again, we could make it home and get some help to find this thing. If it's just me and you, we could get trapped down there."

"We can't risk someone else finding it. It has to be protected. The wrong kind of person could do awful, terrible things if they got their hands on it."

"Okay, then. If you're so smart, what are we going to do with the sphere if it really is in there?"

"We'll need two wishes. One wish to return all the Woodlizards to normal, and another one wish to return everyone home."

"Okay, so everyone ends up back home safely. What about the sphere? What happens to it once we've made our wishes?"

"I haven't figured that out yet," said Trey.

"Well, before we start worrying about what to do with the sphere, we have to find the thing first." Waylon peered into the hole and then turned to Trey. "Uh, you first."

19

Trey eased into the hole, something he thought he couldn't do earlier that day.

Then it was something I could have done, now it's something I have to do, Trey thought. He hadn't been too fat, only unsure.

Now he was definitely scared.

A current of fear circulated through his body, and cold beads of sweat dotted his forehead. He felt around the edge of the opening, searching for the same spiders that had crawled all over him before. Nothing there. Looking down, everything became completely black a few feet away. He lowered himself into the darkness.

"After we've changed everyone back to normal," Waylon said, "we could get one of them to wish everyone home, but leave one person behind. This one person could wish the sphere away forever, and it wouldn't ever be a problem again."

"You can't wish for the sphere to change or to do something it's not already doing. It stays where it is and what it is." Trey dropped his foot through a blanket of spider web. He instantly felt little things crawling on his leg, and he shook it furiously. "SPIDERS. THERE'S TOO MANY SPIDERS. LET ME OUT."

But when he tried to scramble out, Trey lost his footing.

He fell, landing hard on something flat.

He couldn't breathe for a second, his wind knocked out.

"TREY! TREY! ARE YOU ALL RIGHT?" Waylon called down.

Trey couldn't see anything. He thought he was dead.

His hand dug into the surface under his rear, and came up with dirt. The ground felt soft, even a bit moist. It had cushioned Trey's fall, saving his life.

He slowly got to his feet. Though his entire body hurt, nothing was broken. Trey sat for a few seconds and listened to Waylon.

"TREY? ANSWER ME. ARE YOU OKAY?"

"Yeah," Trey finally answered.

"WHAT DO YOU NEED?"

"Light!"

Silence.

After a few seconds, Trey wondered if the older boy had left him. Then he heard his voice once more.

"Stand clear," Waylon said.

Trey couldn't see where clear would be, but moved to his left anyway.

A fiery ball dropped down the hole and onto the cave floor.

Trey was startled at first, then realized, *of course, Waylon was a Boy Scout. He probably has waterproof matches.*

Trey grabbed the torch, then turned to see where he had landed.

He screamed out loud when he saw someone staring back at him.

20

"WHAT IS IT? WHAT'S DOWN THERE?" Waylon yelled.

Trey caught his breath.

It had looked like someone was in there.

What Trey saw was his own reflection.

"It's a piece of rock. It's smooth and glassy, like a mirror. I saw myself in it, and I thought it was someone else."

"Then it's safe to come down?"

"I don't know about safe, but you can come down," Trey said. Then he approached the rock and picked it up.

It was about the size of a pineapple. Trey figured he must have knocked it loose when he fell.

Trey heard Waylon climbing down, grumbling as he went. Then Waylon suddenly slipped.

Waylon landed on his good ankle and

rolled on the dirt. He got up quickly, and hit his head on the cave ceiling.

"In the middle, where I am, you can stand up," Trey told him.

"Is that what scared you?" Waylon asked and walked over to look at the rock. Trey nodded as Waylon examined it further. "That's just the material of the rock burnt into glass on the surface by lava. It's common enough."

Trey had other ideas.

"This is the only rock of its size in here, and it looks like it's been chiseled. I think someone left it here."

"Thomas?" Waylon asked.

"Maybe. If he did, he would have a reason." Trey looked at where he had fallen.

In the wall beside his landing spot, a niche had been carved. Trey walked over, and placed the rock inside. "Perfect fit."

Waylon opened his mouth, then moved closer to take a look. As he did, a green ray of light beamed into the room, striking the mirror side of the rock.

"Where's that coming from?" asked Trey.

Waylon looked. "There's another opening in this corner of the cave."

Could this be a trap, or the trail leading them to their prize?

"Let's follow it," said Trey.

21

Waylon led the way this time, carrying the torch.

As he passed beyond the hole, he interrupted the beam of light. When he moved out of the way, the beam returned. Trey moved his hand through the ray.

Beam.

No beam.

Beam.

Trey stopped playing with it and went on through. When he reached the other side, things started to make sense.

He saw a rock, exactly like the one he had found before, on the other side. This one, however, caught one beam from a point beyond and shot one back from where they had come.

"What do you think it is?" Waylon asked.

"I don't know. Maybe it's to lead us through the caves."

"Or maybe it's to let someone or something know we're coming."

They went on, and soon, as they suspected, came upon another rock.

The torch finally flickered and died. Waylon shook the stick, then used it to grope his way through the darkness.

"I can't see a thing."

"Follow the beams," Trey said.

They moved through the darkness with nothing but a thin ray of green light to show them the way. Every few seconds, one of them would brush in front of the beam, and they would be in complete blackness. They would stop, find the light again and continue. Soon Trey felt cold air blow across his arms and legs.

Waylon stopped ahead of him.

"I can't feel the walls anymore."

"We must be in a big room," Trey guessed. "It's drafty. Lots of air in here."

"Trey, look where this beam ends."

Trey saw that the beam ended fifty yards ahead. It struck something that projected three other beams. As they approached it, Trey could see it was an iron box.

Waylon reached out to touch it.

"It's a box, all right. With three holes carved in it. The lights coming from what's inside."

"Open it," said Trey.

Waylon hesitated. "I've seen movies like this. This box could be booby-trapped or something."

Trey moved in. "Let me open it then."

He put his hands at the side of the box. It vibrated in his hands.

Trey's eyes widened and he couldn't stop the grin from spreading across his face.

"We've found it! We've found the sphere!"

22

The instant Trey opened the container, a brilliant green light flooded the cavern.

It was the sphere.

An emerald globe with visible energy washing around inside it.

Its surface felt solid, but smooth like marble, and it vibrated to the touch.

A marvelous feeling swept through Trey. He could do anything. Anything in the world. With one touch of the sphere, he could have it all. He, stood, head back, lost in the light. He could have stayed in its power forever.

"NO WAY. I CAN'T BELIEVE IT," Waylon yelled. He seemed *overexcited*.

"I know. Awesome isn't it?"

"NO. LOOK BEHIND US!"

Trey snapped out of his trance. He

whipped around.

What he saw made his heart drop.

The light reached into every inch of the cavern, revealing the path the boys had taken. They had crossed on a sort of bridge that looked only twelve inches wide. It stood over a drop into total darkness. If he or Waylon had taken one step to the side, they would have fallen to their deaths.

"I can't believe we were so lucky..."

Trey heard a chirping sound.

Then Waylon screamed, looking at something over their heads.

Trey looked up, and saw a horrifying sight.

Bats.

Hundreds of them.

Before Trey or Waylon could get out of the way, the winged terrors dropped from the ceiling.

They filled the air, diving and striking at the two boys.

Waylon lost his balance and fell over the side of the narrow bridge.

Even through all the bats' shrill screams, Trey heard Waylon.

"HELP! TREY, HELP ME!"

Waylon held onto the side of the path. He hung there in mid air.

The bats knocked over the box, and the sphere came rolling out. It stopped near the edge of the drop.

Trey moved toward it.

"TREY, I'M SLIPPING! I CAN'T HOLD ON, MAN!"

Giving the sphere one last despairing look, Trey turned again to Waylon.

The bats swarmed down on everything. Even through that, Trey could see Waylon losing his grip on the bridge.

His fingers slipped.

Trey leaped and caught his arm. He held him there.

Out of the corner of his eye, Trey could see the sphere edging closer to the abyss.

He found the strength he needed. With a mighty grunt, Trey yanked the older boy up onto the path to safety.

Then he dove for the sphere.

But before he could reach it, someone else got to it first.

Someone with bony hands.

"THOMAS!" Trey exclaimed.

Picking the sphere up, the old soldier turned and swatted at the bats showering down on him. He reached for the box, and placed the sphere inside. As soon as he closed the lid, the bats' assault ended.

A few straggler bats still swooped through the air, but the rest were gone.

Trey got to his feet. He looked over at Waylon, who moaned quietly to himself as he rose.

Trey started toward Thomas.

Suddenly, the skeleton man pulled a gun from a holster on his back and pointed it at Trey.

"Stay back," he growled.

Trey froze.

"Thomas, what's going on?"

"No one may touch the sphere!"

"I-I thought the Woodlizards got you. I came here to find the sphere and guard it myself."

"You lie, boy. No one guards the sphere but me. No one else ever has."

"Okay, okay. I came to find the sphere to save my friends and get us out of here, okay? So don't shoot."

Thomas pointed the barrel at Waylon, limping their way.

"Who's he?"

"A friend. He's helping me. You can trust him," Trey pleaded, his heart hammering against his ribs.

"I can't trust anyone," Thomas said. He pointed the gun at Trey again. "Especially now. The hiding place has been contaminated. You know the sphere is here. And there's a good chance the Woodlizards will find out where you are."

"How?" Trey asked.

"There are other entrances to these caverns. The Woodlizards know your scents now. They'll find you. Now be quiet and let me think."

"Thomas, you can't hurt us. You saved me. I thought you gave your life for mine."

"I'm immortal. I couldn't give my life if I wanted to, but that doesn't mean I would let those

Things tear me apart. I dug my way back underground. I've been holed up in my caves."

"Your caves?"

"Yes, my caves. I dug them. Well, the connecting tunnels, anyway. It's what I've done with my days for the past two hundred years. I've made a labyrinth inside this mountain that's so complex, you could never find your way through it. That's why it's the perfect place to hide the sphere."

Something clicked in Trey's head.

"The rocks! The shiny ones that reflect the light rays. That's how you found your way around."

"It's a warning system too, isn't it?" Waylon asked.

Thomas once again turned the gun towards Waylon, who kept inching closer. Waylon had not spoken to him directly before, and it seemed to make Thomas nervous. It made Trey even more nervous.

"It's a guiding device and, yes, a warning system. I had a rock inside the fort. If the light stopped reflecting, I knew something had happened to the sphere. I managed to crush that rock when the Woodlizards attacked."

"So what are you going to do to us, Thomas?" Trey asked.

"I am not sure, but I can't let you leave now."

Something sailed past Trey and struck Thomas' bony hand, knocking the gun out of its fingers.

Waylon's stick.

The old firearm landed on the ground.

Before Trey could react, Waylon had jumped onto Thomas and the two were locked in a desperate struggle.

25

Waylon moved quicker than Trey thought possible. The force of his impact knocked them both to the ground, and a few pieces of Thomas broke off.

Trey jumped for Thomas' gun, and whipped around to find that the tide of the battle had turned.

Thomas stood up, holding Waylon in the air with one bony hand. Even as Waylon continued to punch the skeleton in the head, Thomas threw him to one side.

He landed by the sphere's box.

Thomas started toward him.

"Thomas, stop!" Trey yelled, and pointed the old dusty firearm toward the skeleton.

Thomas looked at Trey, and then kept walking toward Waylon.

"I can touch this sphere before you can grab me."

Waylon grabbed the box.

"And what are you going to want from it?" Thomas asked angrily, moving closer.

"WAYLON - WE NEED YOUR WISH TO GET HOME!" Trey yelled.

"YOU CAN WALK HOME. I'm going to take care of Mr. Bones, here."

Thomas stopped. "Careful what you wish for, boy. You just might get it."

Waylon lifted the top of the box and held his hand directly over the glowing sphere.

"Back up," he said to Thomas.

The gun was heavy in Trey's hand. This had turned into a standoff. Trey didn't know who to trust, the undead soldier or the bully who held all the power in the world.

Trey had thought Thomas was his friend, but now the skeleton placed the protection of the sphere over that friendship. He didn't know what Thomas would do to him in the end.

Waylon had bullied Trey for years. He'd saved his life that night, but Trey had also saved his, more than once. The sphere had obviously corrupted him, breaking the line of trust Trey had invested in the bully that night. He wanted the sphere's power and didn't care what happened to Trey.

In either situation, Trey came out the loser, unless he did something now.

But what?

As he considered his options, a Woodlizard entered the cavern.

26

Trey pointed his weapon at the beast.

"Kevin? Doug?" he asked.

The Thing didn't answer. It came at Trey, carefully keeping its footing on the narrow path.

Trey closed his eyes, and pulled the trigger. Nothing.

He opened his eyes to stare at the gun, and, horrified, saw the Woodlizard leaping into the air ready to pounce.

From out of nowhere, Thomas tackled the beast, and both creatures hit the floor.

Thomas' legs broke off.

The Woodlizard got to its feet, but it was too close to the edge of the abyss. Losing its balance, it fell over the side.

It howled all the way down, sounding like a blaring bull horn at first, and then a whistling teapot as it got closer to the bottom. Then nothing.

Trey ran over to Thomas, who was spread all over the ground, legless. He'd managed to push himself up with his arms.

"I used all of my gunpowder when they attacked the fort."

Before Trey could say a word, he saw two more Woodlizards invade the cave.

Trey looked at Waylon.

"Waylon, wish them back to normal! I'll wish us home!"

"No way."

Trey stared at him, terrified.

"What?"

"Those things have been after me all day and night. Who cares about them? I'm the one who's suffered. I'm the victim, not them. So I'm going to get something out of this. I WANT COMPLETE CONTROL."

"WAYLON, DON'T!" yelled Trey.

"Don't worry, Trey. You can be part of my new gang!"

Waylon reached toward the sphere as the Woodlizards moved in.

"Don't do it, boy!" Thomas shouted. "Those like you turn to stone when they touch the sphere."

Waylon stopped to look at him, "Yeah. Right."

He hesitated, then grabbed the sphere out of the box and held it over his head.

He instantly turned to stone.

Trey thought, *Thomas said that on purpose, so Waylon would be thinking about it when he touched the sphere and - bam - he turned to stone.*

The sphere fell from Waylon's petrified hands, and rolled over the edge of the drop.

One of the Woodlizards jumped for it, but missed, and fell with the sphere down into the total darkness.

The last Woodlizard seemed confused. The pursuit of the sphere was its reason for living. It was unsure what to do next.

"Trey," Thomas whispered. "Pick me up. Let's get out of here."

"But what about Waylon?"

"There's nothing you can do for him now."

Trey grabbed all the pieces of Thomas he could find. "Where to?" he asked.

"Back behind the sphere's pedestal. There's a hole. It's our only way out!"

Trey found the tunnel and darted through it. The Woodlizard chased after them.

27

"He's catching up!" Trey cried.

"KEEP RUNNING!" Thomas commanded.

Trey heard the pads on the bottoms of the Woodlizard's feet smack against the stone floor. They came closer.

"Where?" Trey gasped.

"To the fort! There's still a chance of saving the sphere!"

"How?"

Before Thomas could answer, Trey stopped running.

In front of them, he saw the glowing red eyes of another Woodlizard.

Trey yelled in desperation.

"Beside you!" Thomas yelled.

To Trey's right there was a crack in the cave wall. Not a large one, but maybe, just maybe, it might be large enough.

Trey didn't hesitate for a second. Holding Thomas in front of him, he dived into the fissure.

It was tight...oh, so tight. Trey squirmed and wriggled, forcing himself further into the crack. He still heard the Woodlizards behind him, almost at the hole. He squirmed even harder.

The rock scratched his face and hands, but Thomas urged him forward. He had to make it! The Woodlizards were at the crack now, hissing and spitting, reaching to grab him with their hideous claws. One more foot to go. One more mighty shove.

There! He was through the crack, into a small opening in the rock. But where to now? Nowhere to go! They were stuck there.

Then Trey looked up.

"A light..." he breathed.

Thomas looked up, too. "You're right, boy. It is. It is!"

The crack opening extended all the way to the surface. Another storm brewed over the forest, and its lightning pierced the darkness below.

Thomas reached up to feel the rock wall just above them.

The opening narrowed a little above

them, but then expanded.

"If we can squeeze through, it'll be a clean climb to the top."

"Thomas I can't! I can't do it!"

Thomas shot his hand up and grasped the first niche in the rock he could find.

"A skinny kid like you? Sure you can. Grab onto my spine. It's strong enough to hold!"

Trey worked his way into position, gripped Thomas' backbone, and let the old soldier lead the way.

Thomas actually grunted as he climbed the first few inches.

Trey made a lot more noise. It felt as if someone had tried to fit him into a soda bottle. He screamed all the air out of his lungs and couldn't breathe at all as Thomas yanked him through the gap. One long scrape marked Trey from head to toe.

The Woodlizards shrilled, reaching as far through the crack as they could, trying to grab Trey before Thomas lifted him out of range. When they realized they had no chance of getting to them, the Woodlizards broke off, and ran back into the cave, screaming in rage.

"They've gone," Trey gasped.

"To get help," said Thomas. "We have to get to the top before they do."

As Thomas climbed, small rocks and dust and dirt fell into Trey's face. He continuously spit things out of his mouth, but managed to yell when one of Thomas' ribs broke. The old soldier showed no sign of pain, and Trey managed to keep control. He thought of Thomas as a very old house. Some parts remained strong and stable, while others had rotted away.

As they approached the top, Thomas stopped his ascent.

"What is it? What's wrong?" Trey asked.

"I'm listening for them. I don't want to climb out into an ambush."

They stayed silent for a few more seconds. Trey heard nothing. Thomas lifted them to the top.

Darkness.

The thunder rumbled to welcome them.

Trey watched Thomas roam around on his hands, scanning the woods for their enemy.

"Do you see them?" Trey asked.

"No. But they'll be here soon. Hurt bad?"

"I can walk."

"You'll have to run. And this time, you'll carry me."

28

Trey got to his feet, wincing in pain. He picked up Thomas and put him on his back. Thomas quickly put his arms around Trey's neck.

"Let's go," Thomas whispered, "but try to stay quiet."

Trey took off.

The pain settled in within the first hundred yards. Being pulled through the rocks had shaved a layer of skin off Trey's front and back. Just running made it sting.

At first, Trey only heard the sounds of his feet running, and the thunder booming that he hoped overwhelmed the crashing of his footsteps. Then he felt Thomas' skull ease up closer to his ear.

"Remember when I told you about my well? There's an underground river at the bottom of that drop where the sphere fell. That river spills into the pool where I dug my well. It's a long shot, but the sphere might have washed in there," Thomas whispered.

Trey shot back, "Why do you even care about the sphere? If it's gone, you don't have to guard it anymore."

"The sphere can't be destroyed. I'll always be guarding it, even if I lose it now and then."

"What about the Woodlizards? They took over the fort. They'll be there."

"I have a plan, but we must get there first. Be quiet, and go over that hill to the right."

"I won't be quiet. When we find the sphere, then what? What about me? What about my friends?"

"TREY-WATCH OUT!"

Trey screamed.

A pair of red, glowing eyes moved through the air toward him.

Trey ducked on instinct alone, and the beast flew over him and rolled to the bottom of the hill.

Jumping up to run, Trey turned to find more trouble.

Woodlizards stood at the base of the other

side of the hill. They came up after him.

Trey braced himself.

"WAIT..."commanded the Woodlizard who jumped at them.

The beasts stopped their attack.

Trey just stood there, shaking.

Thomas studied the beast giving orders.

"Fitzgerald McCree," he said, simply.

29

Through his panic, it took Trey a second to remember where he'd heard the name.

Fitzgerald McCree. The pirate who had ambushed Thomas so long ago. The leader of the Woodlizards - of course!

"We've taken the fort, yet ye were runnin' back to it. Were ye gonna take us on, Thomas? Ye and the boy?" the McCree lizard asked.

Thomas didn't respond.

"I know what happened to the sphere, but ye know somethin' too, don't ye, Thomas?"

Lightning crashed in the sky, followed by bellowing thunder. Trey noticed the Woodlizards getting anxious.

"Why don't you just end this here?" Thomas said to McCree. "If I knew the where-abouts of the sphere, I'd never tell you."

"The boy will tell me," the Woodlizard leader proclaimed.

Trey looked at McCree. He tried to control his shaking but he felt something strong between fear and anger. McCree was a terrible monster, the scariest looking Woodlizard he'd seen yet, but how dare he think Trey would betray Thomas and the sphere?

The beast stood still. If he felt nervous about the storm, he didn't show it. He simply waited for Trey to respond.

Trey stood mute.

McCree continued, "I'll have someone wish ye home. Ye and yer friends. Safe at home. Warm in yer beds. All for tellin' me where the sphere is."

"W-Where are my friends?" Trey asked with a shaky voice.

"At the fort, keeping watch. They're waitin' on you. And Wolf and Blade're behind you, hoping you'll make the right decision."

Trey glanced over his shoulder.

"I've already got my wish. No more Waylon Burst," a Woodlizard chuckled. Trey recognized the voice as Wolf's.

"Come on, Trey, make up your mind,"

another urged, and Trey assumed it to be Blade.

Trey looked back at McCree, who awaited his decision.

"Tis a shame about poor Count Nefarious. Almost had the sphere in his claws, he did. Then he took that spill off the cavern ledge. Then there's that Waylon boy. You're losin' a lot of friends m'boy. It can end if you tell me about the sphere."

Trey stood up as tall as he could. "No way. Find it yourself," Trey told McCree.

Bad weather blew in over the hill, telling the pirate-turned-monster that the time for games had ended. "Oh, to blazes with this," snapped Fitzgerald McCree. "We've no time left. Make him one of us, and then he'll sing like a bird!"

Lightning struck again.

Thunder blared.

Rain fell.

As the Woodlizards attacked, the storm moved in.

They'd waited too long. Now they were caught in the downpour.

The Woodlizards ran about for cover, howling, and bumping into one another in confusion.

McCree jumped in the air, only to land beside Trey and Thomas, writhing in terrible spasms, and shrieking horribly.

Smoke came from his skin.

A deafening howl came from his throat.

His scales bulged up into bubbles, then burst, letting green liquid run down to the ground.

Melting. Fitzgerald McCree was melting.

"I - WANT - THE - SPHERE!" he cried.

Amazingly, he got to his feet. While the other Woodlizards rolled around in agony and ran in circles, McCree stood up and prepared to launch an attack.

30

Trey made a break for it.

Wolf-lizard and Blade-lizard found the strength to give chase with Fitzgerald McCree, who shakily bounded off the hill after Trey and his old foe, Thomas.

Trey heard them behind him. Some shrieked in anger and some out of pain.

Thomas' tone was frantic. "Do you see that hill in the distance? There's a drop off on the other side. Beyond that drop is the fort. If you'll recall, I crawled out of the ground to pull you into my fort when we first met. The hill's full of those holes. We'll dive into one that's close to the well."

"And if the sphere's not there?"

"The Woodlizards are so mad, you'll probably end up looking like me."

Trey didn't want to think about that. Instead, he thought about grabbing the sphere and wishing everything back to normal. He thought of all the damage he could undo if he could just get his hands on that glowing magic.

But he didn't have it yet.

The rain pounded down now, and the screams from behind Trey sounded agonizing. The Woodlizards must have been falling apart as they pursued him.

Trey hurt too. His injuries burned him worse than ever. His whole body stung so badly that tears welled in his eyes.

"They're on us, Trey!" Thomas warned.

Trey cleared his eyes by opening them wide. He saw a familiar sight.

Wolf ran on one side of him, Blade on the other. Just as they had in the mud trench earlier that day. Only Wolf and Blade looked a little different now.

The smoke from their skin trailed off behind them as they ran. Their glowing eyes dimmed and brightened again like dying light bulbs. The green scales that covered them bubbled up so fast, their skin appeared to be sizzling.

Trey wondered if he could outlast them.

He tripped and fell flat on his face.

Blade-lizard jumped for him in mid-air, and missed his target completely when Trey fell. The Woodlizard smacked into the dirt and rolled next to Trey.

Something grabbed Trey's leg. He looked down to see the cuff of his pants clenched in Wolf-lizard's teeth.

Trey grabbed onto the Blade-lizard and crawled over him, yanking his foot wildly. His foot flew free of Wolf-lizard's mouth, bringing Wolf's teeth along with it. Everything about the beasts must have weakened in the rain.

Trey crawled over the dazed Blade, then plodded up the hill, watching for other Woodlizards.

When the rest of the pack, Fitzgerald, Pogue, and Morley, hit the hill, they had as much trouble as Trey. Disintegrating by the second, scaling a hill proved almost impossible.

But Trey knew they had been after the sphere too long to let a little rain stop them. They continued the chase, and even gained on Trey as he reached the top of the hill.

"We're almost there!" Thomas yelled.

Anxiously, Trey reached up to grab some

grass to help pull himself over the top.

It came out in his hand.

He lost his balance, and fell backward, into the oncoming pack.

They attacked him.

From every direction, Trey saw snarling, dripping teeth, green scales, and red eyes.

He went crazy, swinging in every direction, and kicking whatever his hands missed.

He felt Thomas scratching about underneath him.

Trey rolled over and Thomas slugged the first Woodlizard he saw (Fitzgerald).

Screaming, Trey broke free and ran full throttle down the other side of the hill.

The Woodlizards followed, preparing to pounce when Trey slowed at the drop off.

He didn't slow down.

31

Trey ran at full speed off the edge of the drop and flew through the air.

Waving his arms and legs about as he soared, he stiffened when he approached the ground, hit it, and went through it.

He had jumped right through one of Thomas' holes.

Through it he went, into a small curving tunnel. Mud formed from the rain and Trey slid through the earth-crusted tube like a water slide.

It took only seconds to get to the bottom, but Trey emerged traveling at high speed, and slammed into the outer cavern's rock wall.

Something broke and scattered.

Thomas.

It took Trey a few seconds to make the connection, but when Thomas' skull rolled in front of him, he realized all too well what had happened.

"THOMAS!" he screamed.

"No time to cry! Get us to the well!" Thomas' skull replied.

Trey gathered his wits, picked up the skull and made his way through the caves underneath the fort.

"Go left - now right!" Thomas directed. "There, beyond that opening, are stairs I've carved into the rock, leading down to the well!"

As Trey reached the access, the blackness on the other side made him stop. He couldn't see a thing, especially the stairs.

"Go! Go! What are you waiting for?" Thomas urged.

Suddenly, Trey saw two glowing eyes in front of him, growing larger.

A Woodlizard burst from the darkness.

Trey leaped to the side of the opening to avoid being tackled.

The Woodlizard hit the ground, spun around and hissed at him.

"HOW CAN YOU BE HERE? McCREE SHOULD HAVE TAKEN CARE OF YOU!"

The voice. Kevin-lizard. It moved to attack.

"Kevin- Kevin don't!" Trey pleaded, then backed up, and fell into the shadowed void.

He dropped into the dark, and wondered if he'd fall forever.

He didn't.

Something grabbed him by the shirt.

"I'll turn you into one of us, then you won't have to die," Doug told him. Doug-lizard had snatched him from an uncertain fate. Trey could only guess Doug held him with his claw, suspending him and Thomas in midair.

Trey continued his plea. "Doug, you don't have to do it! There's still a chance."

"Don't beg those beasts for anything," said Thomas, whose eyesockets served as finger holes in Trey's tight grip.

"There's still a chance. Really!" Trey begged.

"Oh yeah? What is it?"

32

What happened next gave Doug an answer to his question.

A green glow spread through the room.

Trey could see!

He hung twenty feet over what had to be the well; a giant hole carved into the rock below, about two yards in diameter.

Trey could see the underground river below it. Jutting from the water were rocks, which broke the underground river up and collected things that floated in it.

In the center of the rocks lay the sphere.

It shocked Doug so badly he lost his grip.

Trey and Thomas fell.

They landed hard on a rocky lower ledge.

A crack and a fiery pain in his leg. Trey knew he'd broken something.

He hollered in agony, pressing his head into a rock, his pain unbearable. Hearing something roll beside him, he turned his head as he started to bawl.

Thomas had bashed into a rock beside Trey, and lay in the dirt, sporting a hole the size of another eyesocket.

The old soldier still kept his wits.

"TREY! TREY-HOW BAD IS IT?"

Trey had cried out so much, he lost his breath. He desperately tried to catch it.

"My leg - I broke my leg!"

He rolled over to lie on his back, and the pain shot through once more like lightning.

He screamed again.

He saw the Doug and Kevin Woodlizards moving back and forth on the ledge above them. They didn't seem to know what to do.

Trey was bawling. "I'm going to die here!" he choked.

"NO YOU'RE NOT!" Thomas shouted. "STAY HERE WITH ME, TREY! DON'T GIVE UP YET!"

Thomas' words trailed off. Trey just wanted to shut everything out of his mind and fall into a deep sleep.

Then he felt something dripping on his face.

Trey opened his eyes and through his tears saw Fitzgerald McCree, looking down on him from above.

The rain had done a number on him. Through the bubbly green gel that covered him, Trey could see a hint of bone. McCree's eyes didn't glow anymore. He had trouble standing; his legs could hardly support the weight, and his own shaking loosened Fitzgerald's green jelly shell. Trey realized what had dropped onto his face as another bead plopped on his forehead.

Fitzgerald wheezed and turned to the other two.

"Go get him, and the sphere."

33

Doug-lizard and Kevin-lizard started down, but the Woodlizards who had followed McCree in from outside pushed ahead of them. They looked as bad as their leader, and just as shaky.

They stopped when they reached the steps.

Thomas had carved the steps so narrow, the beasts couldn't use them.

The Woodlizards would have to climb down.

Thomas whispered to Trey. "Now, Trey, listen to me. If they get the sphere, it's over. It's all over. We do have an option, but it'll be up to you."

"I can't - I can't..." Trey whimpered.

"You have to. You can't run. They know that. But we can still make sure they don't get the sphere."

"I don't want to be a Woodlizard."

"Don't worry about that. If this works,

they'll hate you!"

"Thomas..."

"Curse it boy! Look at defeat as opportunity! You can change things in a second if you're sharp!"

Trey turned his head to watch the Woodlizards, carefully making their way down the ledge just a few yards away.

"Hurry!" McCree yelled. He seemed to be falling apart faster by the second. "We need that sphere or we're finished."

Dread washed through Trey, "I've got to do something."

"You've shown courage my boy. You've been the only ally I've had in two hundred years, and I'm proud to fall in battle beside you," said Thomas. "On my mark, roll over, and throw me at the sphere. If luck's on our side, I'll hit it. It'll wash down a fall I know of a little farther down, and will never be seen again."

"It can't end like this," muttered Trey.

"It didn't look like it would ever end at all, until you came along," said Thomas.

Swallowing hard, Trey picked Thomas up in his hand, held him tightly, and waited.

The Woodlizards approached.

Trey's mind filled with ideas, things he could've done. If he'd only had another chance. Things just couldn't end like this.

He saw Doug and Kevin peeking over the edge at him and whatever hope they'd had to get home didn't show up in their faces.

Trey knew he had to change things.

Look at defeat as an opportunity.

He could change things in a second if he was sharp.

The Woodlizards landed on the ledge.

Fitzgerald McCree wheezed even louder.

"NOW!" Thomas shouted.

34

Trey aimed, and launched Thomas' skull through the air, striking Fitzgerald McCree right between the eyes.

McCree wobbled, fell off the edge, through the well's mouth, and splashed into the water below it.

A shriek, louder and more cutting than any Trey had heard that night, filled the cavern and held for many, many moments.

"MY BROTHER! MY BROTHER FITZGERALD! " one of the McCree brothers screamed. Trey didn't know which one.

As the Woodlizards leaped down to get their revenge, Trey knew it was time to move.

He pulled himself over to the edge, and with his good leg, propelled himself off the side.

Throwing his hands out in front of him,

Trey dove straight into the well.

The sphere didn't move, but simply bumped against the rocks.

Approaching it desperately, Trey reached out his hand...

And touched it.

With one thought in his mind, he touched the sphere.

One thought.

35

Kevin turned, "What are you talking about? It'll only take about an hour."

Familiar words. Familiar scene.

Kevin.

To the right of him, Doug.

He'd done it.

The fall hadn't killed him.

The sphere had returned him to that very morning when it all began, just where he wanted to be.

Doug and Kevin stared at him for a second.

"What's the matter with you, Trey?" Doug asked. "We have to get out of here. Waylon and his goons will be coming soon."

Trey sat and looked at them. "This is fantastic," he finally said. "Everything's fantastic."

"Trey, now you're just acting plain dorky,"

Doug said.

Trey didn't understand. Why didn't Doug or Kevin realize what had happened?

Unless they didn't remember...

Trey had made the wish on the sphere, so he kept the memories. Everything else was a clean slate.

That must be it, Trey thought.

"So what are you going to do, Trey?" Doug asked again. "Are you going to stay here and let Waylon beat you to death, or are you going with us to Widow Hill?"

His entire body still shook a little, but Trey managed to get to his feet. "There's no way I'm sticking around here," Trey said. "But if you think I'm going to Widow Hill, you're crazy, too."

"Then what?" Kevin asked.

Trey looked over to the hill he had climbed to scan the neighborhood.

"They'll be here any second. We'll need a place to hide. How about behind that dirt hill?"

Suddenly, from a hill a hundred yards away the birds scattered, the flapping of wings filled the air.

Doug gulped in a breath.

Kevin kicked up leaves as he ran into the

Dark Woods, and then abruptly stopped. He turned to look at Trey and Doug, and got his shirt snagged on a branch.

Trey led Doug behind the dirt hill. He saw Kevin panic and rip his shirt free of the branch.

Kevin rushed over to his friends, and hid behind the dirt hill with them. They watched for the enemy.

Waylon and his crew topped the hill and stormed down into the campsite.

Trey thought about what a shame it was that the bullies didn't remember any of what happened. It might've taught them a lesson.

"Where are they?" Count Nefarious asked.

"I heard someone running down here, I know it!" exclaimed Wolf.

"Search around," ordered Waylon.

Trey remembered the bully whimpering as the Woodlizards chased them. No one would ever take orders from Waylon if they saw him like that.

The bullies pillaged the campsite, dumping over things and searching for clues.

"Hey! I found something!" yelled Blade. He pulled a piece of material from Kevin's shirt off of the tree branch. "You guys, I think they ran into the Dark Woods."

"Isn't that Doug kid always babbling about that old fort on Widow Hill?" Wolf asked.

"Yep," said Waylon. "Let's go after them."

"Go after them?" asked Count Nefarious. "To Widow Hill?"

"You bet," answered the king bully. "No one gets away from Waylon Burst."

The henchmen looked at each other, and then accepted their orders like good soldiers.

Waylon's gang entered the Dark Woods, headed for Widow Hill. Woodlizard territory.

Trey smiled. Soon it would be Waylon Burst looking for a place to hide.

And now
an exciting preview
of the next

STRANGE®
MATTER

#5 The Last One In
by Marty M. Engle

"Hold on, Michelle. Let me give it one more crank," Dad called from the boat.

Easy for him to say. My cut chin plunged below the water again, stinging like crazy. I could barely keep my head above water, even with my yellow life jacket.

"Don't feel too bad, Michelle," Erin called, leaning over the side and trailing her finger in the water. "You did pretty good for your first time up. Just remember to let go of the rope next time."

Erin, my older sister, considers herself a waterskiing expert. Actually, she considers herself an expert on everything. Only fifteen and a red-haired master of the world. She talks a lot but does little.

I am Michelle Boyd. I'm thirteen and my hair is a little lighter than Erin's. I talk a lot and do even less than she does. I swore to myself that would change this summer.

Erin flopped over onto her back and crossed her legs, kicking at the sky. The bright yellow towel she was lying on drooped over the edge of the boat and sloshed against the side.

I didn't feel too bad. My first time water-skiing and I stayed up for almost four minutes. That's pretty good, if I say so myself. Next time I have to remember to let go of the rope. There's nothing like getting dragged on your face across a lake. My nose still ran with water.

"Stupid boat," Dad grumbled, pressing the ignition switch again. The boat had given him a lot of trouble this year. It's really not our boat. It belongs to the Keen's next door. They live on Wataga Lake all year. That's gotta be great. We rent a cabin here every summer for a month. The rooms are super big and nice. It's just like a house only better with real log walls and big screened porches and brick barbecues.

Anyway, the Keen's are really nice except for their bratty little blond boy Billy. He's about ten, though he acts like he's five. They spoil him to death. It's Billy this and Billy that. He gets anything he wants. You should see his room. He has every radio controlled vehicle known to man; cars and planes, boats and subs, and even a hover craft. It looks like a boat, but has a giant fan on the bottom. It stays about three inches above whatever it's moving over. It is very cool.

Anyway, all he has to do is whine and it's his. Oh, don't get me wrong. He's not all bad. When I broke my leg up here last summer, he hung around with me every day to keep me from getting bored.

It would help if he didn't act so immature. I'm thirteen, so I've outgrown that kind of behavior. But girls mature faster than boys. All girls except Erin. She acts as immature as Billy does. They pick on each other like five-year-olds.

"Got it!" Dad exclaimed. The boat sputtered once, twice and died.

"Don't got it. Hang in there sweetie." Dad grabbed the manual. His arms glowed red with sunburn. We had been out on the water most of the day.

"Don't worry about me. I'm not going anywhere," I yelled back. The water was greenish-black, and the coldest I could remember it being. But it felt great. It made me feel alive.

Last summer I wouldn't do anything after I broke my leg jumping off rocks into the lake. I moped around and had zero fun, afraid to do anything. I vowed not to let that happen again.

Nothing would stop me this summer. Sometimes you have to dare yourself to do things you normally wouldn't. I'd always been too scared to waterski before but here I was. Treading water. Wet as could be. Stayed up four minutes. I couldn't have been happier.

Suddenly Erin pointed across the lake behind me and screamed.

About the Authors

Marty M. Engle and **Johnny Ray Barnes Jr.**, graduates of the Art Institute of Atlanta, are the creators, writers, designers and illustrators of the **Strange Matter**® series and the **Strange Matter**® World Wide Web page.

Their interests and expertise range from state of the art 3-D computer graphics and interactive multi-media, to books and scripts (television and motion picture).

Marty lives in La Jolla, California with his wife Jana and twin terror pets, Polly and Oreo.

Johnny Ray lives in Tierrasanta, California and spends every free moment with his fiancée, Meredith.

THE SCARIEST PLACE IN CYBERSPACE.

Visit STRANGE MATTER™ on the World Wide Web at
http://www.strangematter.com
for the latest news, fan club information,
contests, cool graphics, strange downloads
and more!

Coming in January

STRANGERS®

An incredible new club exclusively for readers of Strange Matter™

To receive exclusive information on joining this *strange* new organization, simply fill out the slip below and mail to:

STRANGE MATTER INFO •Front Line Art Publishing • 9808 Waples St. • San Diego, California 92121

Name _Aamin McClendon_ Age _11_

Address _____

City _Tucson_ State _AZ_ Zip _____

How did you hear about Strange Matter™?

_____

What other series do you read?

_____

How did you get this Strange Matter™ book?

_____